DATE DUE

OCT 2 9 1991			
NOV 2 7 1991			
JAN 5 '91			
JG			
SEP 2 3 1992			
OCT 0 1 1992 OCT 1 4 1992			
NOV 1 2 1992			
JAN 0 4 1993			

BABA YAGA

A RUSSIAN FOLKTALE

retold by

ERIC A. KIMMEL

illustrated by

MEGAN LLOYD

Holiday House / New York

To Mary and her auntie

E.A.K.

*For Carol who, like the little frog,
gives good advice.*

M.L.

Text copyright © 1991 by Eric A. Kimmel
Illustrations copyright © 1991 by Megan Lloyd
All rights reserved
Printed in the United States of America
First Edition

Library of Congress Cataloging-in-Publication Data

Kimmel, Eric A.
Baba Yaga : a Russian folktale / retold by Eric A. Kimmel ;
illustrated by Megan Lloyd.—1st ed.
p.   cm.
Summary: When a terrible witch vows to eat her for supper,
a little girl escapes with the help of a towel and comb given
to her by the witch's cat.
ISBN 0-8234-0854-X
1. Baba Yaga (Legendary character)—Juvenile literature.
[1. Baba Yaga (Legendary character) 2. Fairy tales.
3. Folklore—Soviet Union.] I. Lloyd, Megan, ill. II. Title.
PZ8.K527Bab   1991   90-39215   CIP   AC
398.2—dc20   [E]

Once upon a time, a wealthy merchant lived in a fine house on the edge of a deep, dark forest. His first wife had died years before, leaving him an only daughter. She was a kind, good-hearted girl named Marina who would have been exceptionally beautiful as well were it not for a great ugly horn growing out of the middle of her forehead. In time the merchant married again. His second wife, a proud, haughty woman, had a daughter of her own named Marusia, whom she thought the loveliest child on Earth, though in truth she was spiteful and lazy. Nonetheless the merchant cherished her as his own. The two girls, Marina and Marusia, grew up together as sisters.

One day the merchant set out on a journey to foreign lands. He promised to return in a year's time. But a year went by without any word from him. Then another, and another. By then his second wife, Marina's stepmother, gave him up for dead.

"Your father is gone, never to return," the stepmother told Marina. "We are poor now. You must learn to do without." She took away Marina's pretty dresses and gave her a ragged smock in their place.

Instead of her warm bed, Marina now slept on the floor between the dog and the cat. From early in the morning until late at night, she worked like a slave.

All she ever heard was, "Marina, sweep the floor!" and "Marina, scour the pots!" and "Marina, why are you so slow?"

But poor as they were, her stepmother and stepsister never dirtied their hands with work of any kind. They wore silken gowns. They slept on feather beds. They ate white bread and cheese. Stale crusts of moldy black bread soaked in water were all Marina ever got to eat.

One afternoon Marina's lazy stepsister Marusia sat up in bed. As she yawned and stretched, she glanced out the window into the yard and saw Marina chopping wood for the stove. Marusia burst into tears. Her mother rushed to her bedside.

"Marusia, my beauty, why are you weeping?"

"Ah, Mother, it is all Marina's fault. That frightful horn! It distresses me so. I cannot bear to look at it."

"You are quite right, my darling. A delicate child such as you should not have to see such things. Dry your eyes, precious. Go back to sleep. Mother will fix everything. I promise that by to-night Marina and her hideous horn will be gone."

The stepmother went out into the yard. "Marina, dear, put down that ax. You have worked hard enough today."

Marina looked up in surprise. Her stepmother had never said that to her before.

"Dear child," the stepmother continued, "your smock is so ragged and dirty. Fetch me a needle and thread. I will sew another one for you."

This surprised Marina even more for, except for slaps and blows, her stepmother had not given her one single thing since her father went away.

"Dear Stepmother," Marina replied, unable to believe her ears, "there is neither needle nor thread in the house. But I can fetch them from our neighbor, if you like."

"Oh, that will take too long, too long, Marina dear," her stepmother said. "I have a better idea. Go visit Auntie-in-the-Forest.
Ask her to lend us what we need."

Now poor Marina shook with fear, for "Auntie-in-the-Forest"
was none other than Baba Yaga, the witch. Even so, she dared
not disobey. She did as her stepmother ordered, and started down
the forest path.

The twisting path wound through dark, gloomy trees. Briars and brambles barred the way. Marina walked for a long, long time. At last, footsore and weary, she stopped to rest beside a forest spring.

"Hello, pretty girl. Where are you going?" a tiny green frog called to her from the middle of the spring.

"I am going to visit Auntie-in-the-Forest to borrow a needle and thread," Marina answered.

"Poor girl, poor girl! Turn back, turn back!" the frog warned. "Your auntie is a wicked witch. She will eat you up."

"I must do what I must do," Marina replied sadly.

"In that case," said the frog, "I will give you some advice. When you arrive at your auntie's house, a birch tree will whistle and moan. Tie a ribbon around its trunk. The gate will creak; pour some oil on its hinges. The dog will bark; give him some meat. The cat will spit and hiss; give her a saucer of milk. When your auntie asks what you want, tell her your heart's desire. Have no fear. If you remember to do these things, all will be well."

"Thank you, kind frog," Marina said. She continued on her way.

In a while she came to a clearing in the woods. There she saw a strange little hut that stood on chicken feet. Baba Yaga sat in the doorway, washing her bony legs. Her teeth were made of iron. Her face looked like a bowl of gray pudding.

"What do you want, little girl?" Baba Yaga asked when she saw Marina coming.

"Stepmother wants a needle and thread to sew me a smock, but I want you to take this horn from my forehead."

"Come closer, my dear," Baba Yaga said. Marina came closer. Baba Yaga plucked the horn from her forehead and stuck it on the wall. "There! Now I have done something for you. What will you do for me?"

"Whatever you like, Auntie," Marina said.

"Go inside my little hut. You will find a kettle on the stove. Fill it with water from the well, then light a fire underneath it. When the kettle boils, call me in." Baba Yaga laughed to herself. As soon as the kettle boiled, she intended to cook Marina for dinner.

Marina went inside the little hut. Baba Yaga's dog barked at her. She gave him a piece of meat from the table. The cat spat and hissed. She filled her saucer with milk. Then Marina found a pot with a hole in the bottom and took it to the well.

On the way the gate creaked. She poured some oil on its hinges. The birch tree whistled and moaned. She tied her hair ribbon around its trunk.

At last she came to the well. She drew up a bucketful of water and filled the pot to the brim, but the water quickly leaked out through the hole in the bottom. Marina drew up bucket after bucket, but the pot remained empty.

At last Baba Yaga called, "Well? Has the kettle boiled?"

"Soon, Auntie, soon," Marina answered. She carried the empty pot back to the house.

When she came through the door, the cat rubbed against her legs. "Dear Cat," Marina cried, "tell me how to get away from here."

The cat meowed. "You are good and kind. You gave me milk. I will help you. Look on top of the kitchen shelf. You will find a towel and a comb. Take them and run. If Baba Yaga comes after you, throw down the towel. It will become a mighty river. If she crosses that river and begins catching up with you, throw down the comb. It will become a dense forest. She will never get through."

Marina reached on top of the shelf. She found the towel and the comb. Hiding them in her apron, she ran out the back door. She passed the dog, but it only wagged its tail. She ran through the gate, but its hinges did not creak. She passed the birch tree, but it did not make a sound. Soon she was far away.

Baba Yaga grew tired of waiting. She wanted her dinner, boiled or not. On stiff, bony legs she hobbled into the kitchen. She found the kettle empty, the stove cold, and Marina gone.

"Where is the little girl I sent to fill the kettle?" she screamed at the cat.

"Far away, far away."

"Why did you not spit and hiss to warn me?"

The cat purred. "That kind girl gave me milk. You only give me water."

Baba Yaga ran out the back door. "Where is that wicked girl, the one I sent to fill the kettle?" she shouted at the dog.

"Far away, far away."

"Why did you not bark to warn me?"

The dog growled. "That kind girl gave me meat. You only give me bones."

Baba Yaga ran out the gate past the birch tree. "Why did you not creak? Why did you not whistle and moan?"

The gate answered, "That kind girl put oil on my hinges. You never bothered to oil them."

"That kind girl gave me a ribbon," the birch tree said. "You never gave me so much as a thread."

In a rage Baba Yaga leaped in her mortar. With pestle and broom she flew after Marina. But Marina saw her coming and threw down the towel. As soon as it touched the ground . . .

it became a mighty river, too deep to go under, too wide to cross over.

Baba Yaga gnashed her iron teeth. She got down on her knees and began to drink. She drank and drank until she drank the river dry. Then she started after Marina.

But Marina saw her coming this time too and threw down the comb. In an instant it became a dense forest full of trees, too tall to climb over, too vast to go around.

Baba Yaga gnashed her iron teeth. Then she began gnawing at the trees. She gnawed and gnawed, but there were too many trees for her to gnaw her way through. In the end she gave up and went home.

Marina went home too. A cavalcade of horses met her at the gate. It was her father, come back at last from his long journey. Marina ran up to him and threw herself into his arms. The merchant could not believe his eyes. Marina was so beautiful she shone like the sun. Her ugly horn was gone.

"What happened to your horn?" the merchant gasped.

"Auntie-in-the-Forest took it away."

"What? Who sent you to Baba Yaga?"

"My stepmother," Marina replied.

The merchant flew into a rage. He turned to his wife and said, "In my house you lacked for nothing. I cherished your daughter as my own. And this is how you repay me: by sending my child to the witch!" He ordered his servants to drive them both from his house.

And so Marusia and her mother found themselves on the road with nothing but the clothes on their backs.

"That wicked girl has cost us everything," Marusia's mother sighed. "But don't despair, my darling. There is hope yet. You must marry a rich merchant, or better still, a prince. To do that you must be beautiful, like Marina. Go at once to Auntie-in-the-Forest. Tell her to make you just like your stepsister."

Marusia grumbled and groaned, but in the end she had to go down the forest path too. Along the way she stopped at the spring.

"Hello, pretty girl. Where are you going?" the tiny frog asked.
"That's no business of yours," Marusia snapped. She threw a
stone at the frog and continued on her way.

In a while she came to the hut on chicken feet. The birch tree whistled and moaned. The gate creaked. The dog barked. The cat spat and hissed. Baba Yaga sat in the doorway with her bony legs crossed in front of her, pulling splinters from her jaws with a clam shell. She looked up when she heard the noise and saw Marusia.

"What do you want?" she said.

"I want to be just like my stepsister," Marusia answered.

"So you shall," said Baba Yaga. Without another word she took Marina's horn from the wall . . .

and stuck it in the middle of Marusia's forehead. There it stayed,
and Marusia had to wear it all the way home.

   If it hasn't fallen off, she has it still.